big & SMALL

Original Korean text by Mi-yeon Anh

Illustrations by Sook-hee Choi

Korean edition © Yeowon Media Co., Ltd.

This English edition published by Big & Small in 2014
by arrangement with Yeowon Media Co., Ltd.

English text edited by Joy Cowley

English edition © Big & Small 2014

ISBN: 978-1-921790-55-3

Printed in Korea

A little bird sang to him,
"Good morning, Peter!"
Peter smiled and waved
at the little bird.

A duck came out the gate.
It wanted to go to the pond
for a morning swim.

8

When the bird saw the duck,
it swooped down and said,
"What kind of bird are you,
if you can't fly?"

The duck quacked at the bird.
"What kind of bird are you,
if you can't swim?"

While the birds were arguing,
something crawled through the grass.

"Look out!" cried Peter
when he saw the cat.

The bird flew up in the tree
and the angry duck quacked
from the safety of the pond.

The cat was very annoyed.
It was walking around the tree
when Peter's grandfather appeared.

Grandfather was also annoyed.
"Peter, what are you doing out here?
I told you not to open the gate.
What if a wolf should come along?"

Peter took no notice
of Grandfather's words.
He wasn't scared of wolves.

Grandfather took Peter by the hand
and locked the gate behind them.

No sooner were they back home,
than a big grey wolf came out of the woods.

When the cat saw the wolf,
it quickly climbed a tree.
The duck quacked with fright
and waddled as fast as it could go.

The wolf was behind the duck.
It came closer, closer…

The wolf swallowed the duck
with one big gulp.

The cat and the bird sat
on different sides of the tree,
shivering with fear.

Peter watched everything
from behind the closed gate.

The wolf walked around the tree,
licking his lips and watching
the frightened bird and cat.

Peter ran quickly to the back yard
and returned with a ladder and a rope.
He put the ladder against the wall
and climbed into the tree.

He whispered to the bird, "Fly in circles around the wolf's head to distract him. Be careful you don't get caught."

The bird flew down, teasing the wolf. The angry wolf snapped at the bird but couldn't catch it.

While the bird was distracting the wolf,
Peter made a lasso with the rope,
and let it hang from the tree.
He caught the wolf's tail
and pulled the rope tight.

The wolf was hanging from the tree
by the tail, and could not get away.

Some hunters who had been following
the trail of the wolf suddenly appeared.
They pointed their guns.

"No! Don't shoot!" shouted Peter.
"The little bird and I caught the wolf.
We don't want you to kill him.
Please take him to the zoo."

Then came a triumphant march. Peter was in front, and following him were the hunters leading the wolf. Grandfather and the cat followed with the bird flying overhead.

"My brave Peter caught this wolf," Grandfather boasted to the people they met on the way.

What happened to the poor duck?
It was still inside the wolf,
quacking loudly and waiting to get out.
In his hurry, the wolf had swallowed it whole.